Dear Parent:
Your child's love of reading starts here!

Every child learns to read in a different way and at his or her own speed. Some go back and forth between reading levels and read favorite books again and again. Others read through each level in order. You can help your young reader improve and become more confident by encouraging his or her own interests and abilities. From books your child reads with you to the first books he or she reads alone, there are I Can Read Books for every stage of reading:

SHARED READING
Basic language, word repetition, and whimsical illustrations, ideal for sharing with your emergent reader

BEGINNING READING
Short sentences, familiar words, and simple concepts for children eager to read on their own

READING WITH HELP
Engaging stories, longer sentences, and l for developing readers

READING ALONE
Complex plots, challenging vocabulary, and high-interest topics for the independent reader

I Can Read Books have introduced children to the joy of reading since 1957. Featuring award-winning authors and illustrators and a fabulous cast of beloved characters, I Can Read Books set the standard for beginning readers.

A lifetime of discovery begins with the magical words **"I Can Read!"**

Visit www.icanread.com for information on enriching your child's reading experience.

I Can Read® and I Can Read Book® are trademarks of HarperCollins Publishers.

The Addams Family: Meet the Family
Printed in the United States of America. No part of this book may be used or reproduced in any manner whatsoever without written permission except in the case of brief quotations embodied in critical articles and reviews. For information address HarperCollins Children's Books, a division of HarperCollins Publishers, 195 Broadway, New York, NY 10007.

www.harpercollinschildrens.com
ISBN 978-0-06-294675-1

19 20 21 22 23 LSCC 10 9 8 7 6 5 4 3 2 1 ❖   First Edition

THE ADDAMS FAMILY

Meet the Family

Adapted by Alexandra West
Pictures by Lissy Marlin

HARPER
An Imprint of HarperCollinsPublishers

This is the Addams Family.

Gomez and Morticia are married.

Their children are

Wednesday and Pugsley.

Uncle Fester is Gomez's

unusual brother.

Grandma is Gomez's

even more unusual mother.

Lurch is the butler.

Thing also helps around the house.

They live in a mansion on a hill.

The Addams Family is a bit different
from other people.
They prefer tricks to treats.

Don't even get them started
on sunshine.
In fact, they think thunderstorms
make the perfect weather.

This is Gomez Addams.

He's a sharp dresser.

Just look at his suit and tie!

Not only is he a sharp dresser,

but he also has a sharp mind.

When he gets an idea,

he gets very excited.

Especially if the idea is terrible.

This is Morticia Addams.

Her style is like her husband's.

She adores her black dress

because it looks great

against her gray skin!

Morticia is the head

of the Addams Family household.

She keeps the other heads in line,

whether they are big or small.

Morticia and Gomez are crazy in love.

Their favorite thing to do together

is dance.

Morticia's favorite dance

is a little dangerous.

She spins Gomez quickly

across the floor.

This is Wednesday Addams.

At thirteen, she is the big sister

in the family.

You will recognize Wednesday

by her braids and cold expression.

Wednesday does things on her own.

She spends a lot of her time

thinking of ways to trick people.

Wednesday is highly intelligent.
She always comes up
with amazing science experiments.
But her science experiments
tend to be creepy.

One time, she brought a dead frog back to life!

This is Pugsley Addams.

He is ten and the only person

in his family with blond hair.

Although he may not

look like his family,

he is just as sinister.

Like his sister, Wednesday,

Pugsley is a bit of a mad scientist.

He likes to build rockets

and things that can really zoom!

But most of all, Pugsley loves it
when his experiments explode!

This is Uncle Fester.

He has no hair

and wears a big, heavy coat.

He comes to visit the Addams Family

from time to time.

He loves to sing.

But his shrill voice

scares people away.

This is Grandma.

She is Gomez's mother.

She loves to go on adventures

all around the world.

She has a reputation

for being good at card playing.

Some people think

she is a rotten cheater.

But they are wrong.

She's actually a very good cheater.

This is Thing.

Thing is a hand.

No . . . really!

Thing is left-handed.

He uses his fingers to walk around.

He doesn't speak,

but he can show you

what he's thinking.

This is Lurch.

He is the family butler.

He answers the door

when people visit the mansion.

Visitors think that his greenish skin

makes him look like a monster.

But he is not as scary as he seems!

Lurch cares for the children.

He's almost like their nanny!

Lurch loves to play the piano.

He is surprisingly good!

Thing loves Lurch's music too.

Even though Thing does not have ears,

he always snaps along.

People think that

the Addams Family is a little scary.

The truth is, they are truly terrifying!

Actually, the only thing

that isn't so spooky

is how much they love each other.

This is the Addams Family.